Published 2015 by Geddes & Grosset, an imprint of The Gresham Publishing Company Ltd, Academy Park, Building 4000, Gower Street, Glasgow, G51 1PR, Scotland

Written by Judy Hamilton.
Artwork by Mimi Everett, courtesy of Simon Girling & Associates, Hadleigh, Suffolk.

ISBN 978-1-910680-51-3

Printed and bound in Malaysia

3 4 5 6 7 8 9 10

# At the Hospital

Geddes & Grosset

Susie and Sam were running home ahead of Mum, racing to the front gate.

"Slow down!" called Mum. Too late!

Sam fell over. Susie tripped over Sam. Crash, bang, wallop! Sam was all right, but Susie hit her head on the garden wall and twisted her wrist.

Susie began to cry. Mum ran up to comfort her but Susie cried and cried.

Mum gave her a hug and took her into the house. She filled a bowl with water and antiseptic and gently cleaned the cut on Susie's head, but it kept on bleeding.

"That's a deep cut," said Mum. "Perhaps we should get it looked at."

Susie was still crying.

"My wrist is so sore!" she said.

Mum looked at Susie's wrist. Sure enough, it was very swollen.

"Oh dear," said Mum, "I think we should phone the doctor."

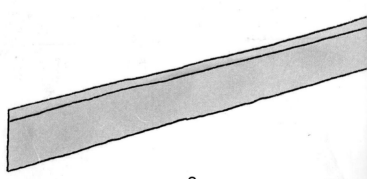

So Mum phoned the doctor and asked him what to do.

"The doctor says that we should go to the casualty unit at the children's hospital, Susie," said Mum. "He thinks you may need an X-ray to see what you have done to your wrist."

A visit to the hospital! Sam thought that this sounded very exciting.

"What's an X-ray?" he asked. "Does it hurt?"

"An X-ray doesn't hurt at all," said Mum. "It's just a special kind of photograph that shows your bones."

Mum drove them to the hospital. They parked the car and went in through big glass doors. It was a very busy place. Doctors and nurses were bustling about. Children, babies and their mums and dads were coming and going all the time. Susie saw a little boy in a wheelchair with a big white plaster cast on his leg. She began to cry again. She was worried.

"Don't cry, Susie," said Mum. "All the doctors and nurses are very nice here. They'll make your arm better, and they will put a proper dressing on your head."

Mum told the woman at the reception desk what had happened to Susie and the woman wrote down all the details. Then they sat down to wait for the doctor. There were toys to play with while they waited, but Susie sat quietly beside Mum.

After a little while, a smiling man in a
white jacket came up to them.

"My name is Jerry," he said, "and I'm a
nurse. I'm going to be looking after you."

He showed them into a cubicle and helped Susie on to the bed. Very gently, he took the dressing off her head.

"That looks sore," he said to Susie, "but I bet you were very brave!"

"Not really," said Sam. "She cried!"

"That's enough, Sam," said Mum, and she gave him quite a stern look.

Quickly and gently, Jerry cleaned up Susie's sore head.

"I'll put a special dressing on this," he said, "to mend the cut and stop it bleeding. That should sort it!"

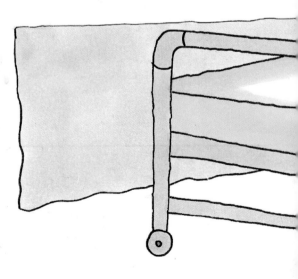

Then a lady in a white coat came in.
"Hello, Susie," she said. "I'm Doctor Liz.
May I look at your sore wrist, please?"

Susie held out her wrist. Doctor Liz
gently gave it a little wiggle.

"I don't think that you have any broken
bones," said Doctor Liz, "but we need
an X-ray, just in case. Jerry will take you
through to the X-ray room when he has
dressed your head. Okay, Jerry?"

"No problem," said Jerry with a smile.

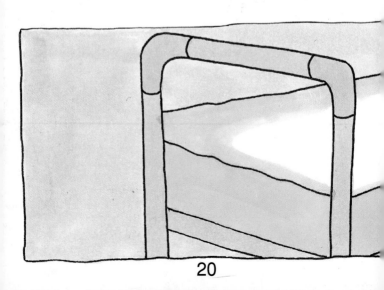

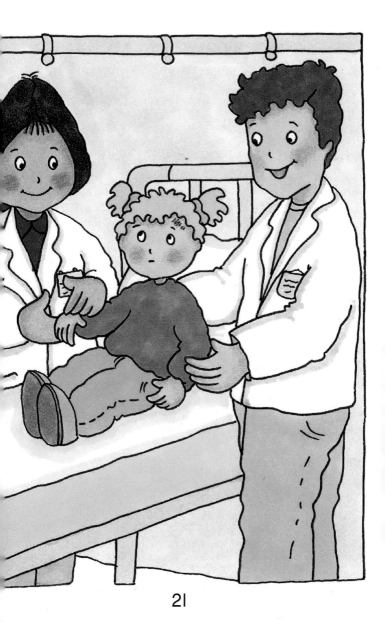

21

Jerry finished dressing Susie's head and then took them all to the X-ray room. Everybody in the X-ray room wore a special apron. There was an apron each for Susie and Mum to wear too. Sam waited outside with Jerry while they took the picture of Susie's wrist.

It was very quick. Susie put her arm on a table under the camera. The woman who took the X-rays went behind a screen. She asked Susie to count to three, and then pushed a button.

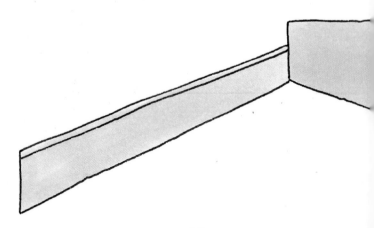

After that, Jerry took them back to the cubicle to wait for Doctor Liz.

Doctor Liz showed Susie the X-ray.

"No bones broken," she said. "You have just sprained your wrist. We will bandage it and put it in a sling. It should feel much better in a few days. Jerry will sort you out. Okay, Jerry?"

"No problem, Doctor Liz," beamed Jerry.

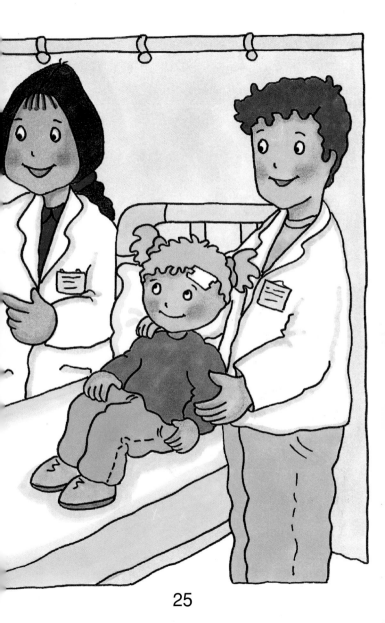

Mum and Sam watched Jerry wrap
Susie's wrist up, just like a parcel, and tie
her arm in a smart white sling.

"That feels better," said Susie, with a
smile.

Jerry gave Susie a "Star Patient" badge, and so that Sam didn't feel left out, he gave him a badge too, which said "Friend Of The Hospital".

Sam felt very proud.

Before they went home, Mum said thank you to Jerry and Doctor Liz.

"No problem," said Jerry, "but don't hurry back!"